WHY ISN'T GOD A GIRL?

A young girl's journey to see the image of God in herself

Diana L. Wilcox

illustrations by Viktoria Skakandi and Earth22 Studio

Dedication

For Nadine, and all children who have a thirst for knowledge, a desire to learn, the courage to ask questions, and the tenacity to keep asking until they get an answer that makes sense.

www.revdianawilcox.com

Acknowledgments

No book is the singular work of the one who envisions it and puts pen to paper. It is the result of a collective effort of people who are willing to give of their time and talent to guide and support the concept until it is fully complete. I give thanks to Alison Curtain, Danielle Treuberg, Dr. Esmilda Abreu-Hornbostel, the Rev. Peter DeFranco, the Rev. Melissa Hall, Candice Whitaker, Sharon Pearson, and Carl Schmidt, for your encouragement and editing.

I thank my parishioners at Christ Church for opening their hearts to the use of inclusive language in worship, and raising up a new generation of children who ask the tough questions, and are unwilling to accept the age-old answers.

I also am grateful to have been raised by two parents who encouraged me to do, and to be, whatever I dreamed, and alongside a brother whose writing talent knows no bounds, and a sister-in-law who quite literally scales mountains. Through them I was blessed with examples of a life without limits.

In all things, I thank God for all that She has done, for all the ways She continues to work in my life, and for the blessing of Her creation.

Preface

One Sunday a few years ago, I was approached during coffee hour by one of our children, Nadine, who at that time was 11 years old. She asked me "Why isn't God a girl?" I immediately responded with "Who said She isn't!" Nadine was both surprised and excited, and ran back to tell her mother. Her reaction told me all I needed to know—the answer was empowering to her. Yet, I knew the answer to my own reply—it is the Church who says She isn't. It is the Church who proclaims God as Father, Lord, and He. I knew something needed to be done to prevent another generation of young people, both girls and boys, from growing up holding only one image of God, born out of patriarchy, and trying to limit a limitless God.

If we are all made in God's image, then girls and women are as much made in that image as boys and men. It is time then for us all to stop the patriarchy and liberate our thinking (as God needs no liberation) to see and experience a much broader understanding of our Creator.

She is certainly hoping we will!
Additional resources for parents and churches may be found in the back of this book.

"In the name of the Father, and of the Son, and of the Holy Spirit," said the priest.

"Amen!" said all the people.

Sophy watched the baptism and thought "Why isn't God a girl?"

"Mom, why isn't God a girl?" asked Sophy.

"That is a good question Sophy."

"Sophy," said her dad, "why don't you ask your Sunday School teacher?"

The Sunday School teacher finished
the story for the day,
"...and that is the story of Jonah and the big fish."

"Miss. Esmilda," Sophy said,
raising her hand to ask a question.
"Yes, Sophy?" her teacher replied.
"Why isn't God a girl?" Sophy asked.

Miss. Esmilda thought for a moment and said, "Well Sophy, we just call God 'Father,' but both girls and boys are made in God's image too."

"I am made in God's image?
I just don't get it,"
Sophy thought as she stared in the
mirror in her room at home.

Sophy decided she would ask her big brother.
"Joey, why isn't God a girl?"
"Girl?" Joey laughed.

"That's easy, because boys are better."
"Besides," Joey said, "that is what the
Bible says."

"Boys are not better!" Sophy said
as she left her brother's room.
Sophy felt Joey was wrong, "But he does have a
point about the Bible," she thought.

"I just don't get it Miles," Sophy said as she played
ball with her best friend.

"Why isn't God a girl?"

"Let's go ask Jacob! He is Jewish.
I bet he knows." said Miles.

"Hi Sophy! Hi Miles!"
"Hi Jacob!"
"Jacob," Sophy said, "I am trying to
find out why God isn't a girl.
Is God a boy in the Jewish church?"

"We worship at the temple, not at a church,"
Jacob replied, "but, yeah, I don't know why.
He just is.
Let's ask Malala! She's Muslim.
She might know."

"Malala, is God a boy in the Muslim church?"
Sophy asked.

"Well," answered Malala, "we call God 'Allah,'
and we don't go to a church. We go to a mosque,
but yes, Allah seems to be a boy."

"Oh, okay," sighed Sophy. "I just want to know why God isn't a girl."

Malala had an idea. "Did you ask Allah?"

"I guess I didn't think of asking God," Sophy answered.

So Miles, Malala, and Jacob follow Sophy to her church, because she said that is where she talks to God best.

"Sophy," Jacob said, "maybe you should try talking to God now." So Sophy began to pray.
"Hi God. It's me, Sophy. These are my friends.
I hear you are a boy, but I am not.
I hear you are Father, but I can't be that.
I hear you are a Lord, but I am told to be a Lady.
I hear I am made in your image, but I do not see it in the mirror...

...I am just a girl, God. Where do I fit in?"
Sophy paused for a moment, and then said,
"I guess that's it. Thanks."

"What did God say Sophy?" asked Miles.
"I don't know. I didn't hear anything,"
Sophy replied.

Just then, the priest of the church appeared.
"Hi Sophy!" the priest said.
"Oh, hi Mother Amy. I hope it's okay to be here.
My friends and I wanted to ask God something."

"Of course," Mother Amy replied.
"May I ask what you asked God?"
"Well..." Sophy started to say.

"She wants to know why God isn't a girl."
said Malala.

"I see," said Mother Amy.
"Who said She isn't?"

"Whoa!"
"Gasp!"
"What?"
Sophy, Miles, Malala, and Jacob
were so surprised.

"You see, each of you are made in God's image,
so God looks like you too Sophy,"
Mother Amy explained.

"Like me?" Sophy asked.

"Or me?" Malala added.
"Me too?" Jacob and Miles asked.

"Yes! All of you are God's children, made in Her, or His, image!
You see, when God was making the world, God wanted Her children to be as wonderfully beautiful as God, in all the ways that could be.

So, God made us all—girls and boys, of many colors, many languages to speak, different sizes and abilities...

...and especially different ways of knowing
God—as Christians, or Jews,
or Muslims, or Hindu, and many other faiths.
All lead to the same God,
making us all sisters and brothers!"

"Wow!" said Sophy.
"Game changer!" said Miles.
"I like it." said Malala.
"I don't think I want any more sisters."
said Jacob.

"But if that is so, why do we only say 'Father' in church?" asked Sophy.

"Well, now you are on to something, Sophy."
Mother Amy replied.
"Perhaps that needs to change.
What do you all think?"
"YES!" Sophy, Miles, Malala, and Jacob shouted.

Sophy said to her friends as they were leaving
the church, "Thanks everybody for
coming with me."
"See you at school tomorrow Sophy!"
they said as they went on their way.

As she went home, Sophy thought about all
that she heard from Mother Amy.
"...who said She isn't?"
"God is also a girl! Wow!!!"

The next Sunday in church...

"Heavenly Mother, you created us in your image, and called us to dwell in your infinite love..."

Mother Amy said, standing behind the altar during communion.

"Mom! Did you hear that?" Sophy whispered,
"She called God 'Mother'!"
Her mother smiled and said softly,
"I did, Sophy! I sure did."

Sophy looked in the mirror again and this time she saw something she didn't see before.

"I really am made in God's image too!" thought Sophy smiling.

Resources for Parents & Sunday School Teachers

Having bought this book, or chosen to use it in Sunday School, you have already shown a willingness, if not eagerness, to break beyond the box into which humanity has tried to place our God, who is beyond our understanding, beyond our human capability to define. Why is this important? This is perhaps the most important question, because the answer underscores the need for our language about God to change. The image of a male God is not wrong, just limiting. It leaves out an entire part of God's essence, and excludes girls, women, and feminine expressing people, from a sense of being connected to the divine Creator. This creates a separation, or really a lowering, of the status of women as related to God. Changing this paradigm is empowering for girls, women, and feminine expressing people, as well as being liberating to all of us in our continued quest to be in the fullest of relationship with God.

Adults

Here are some scriptural sources to provide support to opening our adult hearts to this part of God:

The Bible

Luke 15:8–10: Jesus uses the parable about a woman searching for a lost coin to describe God.

Genesis 1:26: "Then God said, "Let us make humankind in our image, according to our likeness;" While one obvious question is about the use of "our," God did not say, let us make men in our image, and women in the image of something else.

The Holy Spirit

In both of the original biblical languages, Hebrew and Greek, the Holy Spirit was a feminine or gender neutral noun. Ruach in Hebrew, and Pnema in Greek. It was not until the Latin Vulgate bible that the Holy Spirit became Spiritus, a masculine noun. For Trinitarians, if the Holy Spirit is part of the 3 in 1 and 1 in 3, then God is feminine as much as masculine, if God could even be fully defined in these binary terms.

I also recommend She Who Is: The Mystery of God in Feminist Theological Discourse by the Roman Catholic theologian Elizabeth A. Johnson. In this classic work, Johnson reveals the connection of our God-Talk to our sense of identity. Humanity shapes who we believe God to be, but does not shape God, making our names for God more about us than about our Creator. See also The Revelation of Divine Love by Julian of Norwich, and so many more, perhaps taking a course at your local college or seminary.

If you are at a church that is not using inclusive language, speak to the clergy about your desire to have this changed. Often clergy want to include it, but are reluctant to fight the battle with those who will not accept this change. They may find your request a relief. If they do not, consider finding a church that will.

Children

For children, keep it simple. They do not yet have the preset obstacles that would limit their vision of God. Like Sophy in the story, they will thirst for knowledge. To be clear, I am not a parent, so I do not pretend to tell parents how to best raise their children. I will share with you what I have done as a priest in a church where this inclusive language for God has borne fruit in young children.Use feminine language for God when around your children. Do this even more if your church does not. When reading bible stories in Sunday School or at home, if the book uses all male language, change it. Insert some feminine language, or change all the references to female language if your church is not using a mixture of male and female pronouns.

Lift up women of the bible, and reduce the overwhelming emphasis on the male characters. You might start with these examples: Mary Magdalene was NEVER a prostitute. This was an error of Pope Gregory I and perpetuated for centuries. She was a powerful disciple of Jesus, and the first person to whom Jesus revealed himself after he was raised from the dead in every gospel account. Mary, the mother of Jesus, was the chosen one who said "Yes!" to being Theotokos—the God bearer—something no man could ever claim. It was a Samaritan woman who had the deepest theological discussion with Jesus (John 4), and it was an oppressed woman, Hagar, who was the only person in the bible to name God (Genesis 16:13). These biblical models can be liberating to young girls, if only we would speak more about them, and in a less patriarchal way.

In Sunday School, ensure there are pictures of God that are inclusive—both in gender, and also in race. Ask them what God looks like, and use this as a way to expand their vision. Most importantly, encourage them to welcome all images of God, and expand their vision of the God that is undefinable and beyond our imaginations. Finally, read this book in Sunday School and at home to children. Both girls and boys need to hear this message. Here are some good starter questions to ask after reading this book with children:

1. What does God look like?
2. Why does Sophy want to know why God isn't a girl?
3. If God is called Father, who looks like God?
4. If God is called Mother, who looks like God?
5. God is love. Describe love.

That last question is key, as it is impossible to fully define love in much the same way as it is impossible to define God.

I thank you for being willing to raise up a new generation of people who will carry in their hearts a God not limited by human boundaries, empowering children of all genders, races, languages, and ways to love.

It will change the world!

Scan the QR code with your phone camera to find more
titles like this from Imagine and Wonder

Your guarantee of quality
As publishers, we strive to produce every
book to the highest commercial standards.
The printing and binding have been planned
to ensure a sturdy, attractive publication
which should give years of enjoyment.

Replacement assurance
If your copy fails to meet our high standards, please inform us and we will gladly
replace it.

Printed in China by Hung Hing Off-set Printing Co. Ltd.

Scan the QR code to find other
amazing adventures and more from
www.ImagineAndWonder.com